Thomas the Tank Engine & Friends

A BRITT ALLCROFT COMPANY PRODUCTION

Based on The Railway Series by The Rev W Awdry
© Gullane (Thomas) LLC 2002

Visit the Thomas & Friends web site at www.thomasthetankengine.com

All rights reserved. Published by Scholastic Inc.
555 Broadway, New York, NY 10012

ISBN 0-439-33856-5

12 11 10 9 8 7 6 5 4 3 2 1   2 3 4 5 6 7/0
Printed in the U.S.A.
First Scholastic printing, September 2002

This edition is available for distribution only through the direct-to-home market.

A Close Shave

by
The REV. W. AWDRY

SCHOLASTIC INC.

New York   Toronto   London   Auckland   Sydney
Mexico City   New Delhi   Hong Kong   Buenos Aires

So Duck came to Edward's station.

"It's not fair," he complained, "Diesel has made Sir Topham Hatt and all the engines think I'm horrid."

Edward smiled. "I know you aren't," he said, "and so does Sir Topham Hatt. You wait and see."

Duck felt happier with Edward. He helped him with his freight cars and coaches, and sometimes helped foreign engines by pushing their trains up the hill.

But Gordon, Henry, and James never spoke to him at all.

One day, he pushed behind a goods train and helped it to the top.

"*Peep peep!* Good-bye!" he called, and rolled gently over the crossing to the other line. Duck loved coasting down the hill, running easily with the wind whistling past. He hummed a little tune.

***

"*Peeeeep! Peeeeeep! Peeeeeeep!*"

"That sounds like a Guard's whistle," he thought. "But we haven't a Guard."

His Driver heard it, too, and looked back. "Hurry, Duck, hurry," he called urgently. "There's been a break-away, some freight cars are chasing us."

There were twenty heavily loaded freight cars. "Hurrah! Hurrah! Hurrah!" they laughed, "We've broken away! We've broken away! We've broken away!" and before the Signalman could change the points, they followed Duck onto the down line.

"Chase him! Bump him! Throw him off the rails!" they yelled, and hurtled after Duck, bumping and swaying with ever-increasing speed.

The Guard saved Duck. Though the freight cars had knocked him off his van, he got up and ran behind, blowing his whistle to attract the Driver's attention.

"Now what?" asked the Fireman.

"As fast as we can," said the Driver grimly, "then they'll catch us gradually."

They raced through Edward's station whistling furiously, but the freight cars caught them with a shuddering jar. The Fireman climbed back, and the van brakes came on with a scream.

Braking carefully, the Driver was gaining control.

"Another clear mile and we'll do it," he said.

They swept around a bend.

"Oh glory! Look at that!"

A passenger train was just pulling out on their line, from the station ahead.

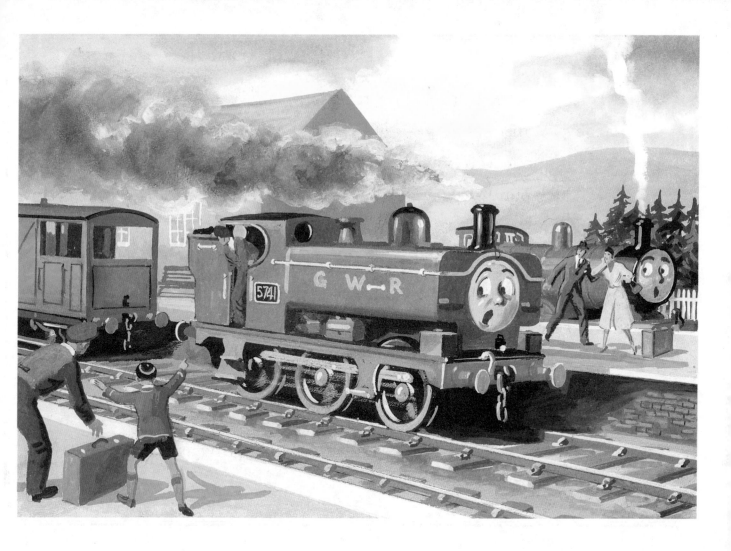

The Driver leaped to his reverser; Hard over—Full steam—Whistle.

"It's up to you now, Duck," he said.

Duck put every ounce of weight and steam against the freight cars.

They felt his strength, "On! On!" they yelled; but Duck was holding them now.

"I must stop them. I *must*."

The station came nearer and nearer. The last coach cleared the platform.

"It's too late," Duck groaned, and shut his eyes.

He felt a sudden swerve, and slid, shuddering and groaning along a siding.

A barber had set up shop in a wooden shed in the yard. He was shaving a customer.

There was a sliding groaning crash, and part of the wall caved in.

The customer jumped nervously, but the barber held him down. "It's only an engine," he said calmly, and went on lathering.

"Beg pardon, Sir!" gasped Duck. "Excuse my intrusion."

"No. I won't," said the barber crossly, "you've frightened my customers and spoiled my new paint. I'll teach you." And he lathered Duck's face all over.

Poor Duck.

Dirty Work

by
The REV. W. AWDRY

SCHOLASTIC INC.

New York   Toronto   London   Auckland   Sydney
Mexico City   New Delhi   Hong Kong   Buenos Aires

When Duck returned, and heard the freight cars singing, he was horrified. "Shut up!" he ordered, and bumped them hard. "I'm sorry our freight cars were rude to you, Diesel," he said.

Diesel was still furious. "It's all your fault. You made them laugh at me," he complained.

"Nonsense," said Henry, "Duck would never do that. We engines have our differences; but we *never* talk about them to freight cars. That would be des—des . . ."

"Disgraceful!" said Gordon.

"Disgusting!" put in James.

"Despicable!" finished Henry.

Diesel hated Duck. He wanted him to be sent away. So he made a plan.

Next day he spoke to the freight cars. "I see you like jokes," he said in his oily voice. "You made a good joke about me yesterday. I laughed and laughed. Duck told me one about Gordon. I'll whisper it . . . Don't tell Gordon I told you," and he sniggered away.

"Haw! haw! haw!" guffawed the freight cars. "Gordon will be cross with Duck when he knows. Let's tell him and pay Duck back for bumping us."

Diesel went to all the sidings, and in each he told different stories. He said Duck had told them to him. This was untrue; but the freight cars didn't know.

They laughed rudely at the engines as they went by, and soon Gordon, Henry, and James found out why.

"Disgraceful!" said Gordon.

"Disgusting!" said James.

"Despicable!" said Henry. "We cannot allow it."

They consulted together. "Yes," they said, "he did it to us. We'll do it to him, and see how *he* likes it."

Duck was tired out. The freight cars had been cheeky and troublesome. He had had hard work to make them behave. He wanted a rest in the shed.

"*Hoooooooosh!* KEEP OUT!" The three engines barred his way, and Diesel lurked behind.

"Stop fooling," said Duck, "I'm tired."

"So are we," hissed the engines. "We are tired of *you*. We like Diesel. We don't like you. You tell tales about us to freight cars."

"I don't."

"You do."

"I don't."

"You do."

Sir Topham Hatt came to stop the noise.

"Duck called me a 'galloping sausage'," spluttered Gordon.

" . . . rusty red scrap-iron," hissed James.

" . . . I'm 'old square wheels'," fumed Henry.

"Well, Duck?"

Duck considered. "I only wish, Sir," he said gravely, "that I'd thought of those names myself. If the dome fits . . . "

"Ha! Ahem!" Sir Topham Hatt coughed.

"He made freight cars laugh at us," accused the engines.

Sir Topham Hatt recovered. "Did you, Duck?"

"Certainly not, Sir! No *steam* engine would be as mean as that."

"Now, Diesel, you heard what Duck said."

"I can't understand it, Sir. To think that Duck of all engines . . . I'm dreadfully grieved, Sir; but know nothing."

"I see." Diesel squirmed and hoped he didn't.

"I am sorry, Duck," Sir Topham Hatt went on, "but you must go to Edward's station for a while. I know he will be glad to see you."

"Beg pardon, Sir, do you mean now?"

"Yes, please."

"As you wish, Sir." Duck trundled sadly away, while Diesel smirked with triumph in the darkness.

Now flip the book over to start another Thomas & Friends adventure.

They were pulling the freight cars away when Sir Topham Hatt arrived. The barber was telling the workmen what he thought.

"I do *not* like engines popping through my walls," he fumed. "They disturb my customers."

"I appreciate your feelings," said Sir Topham Hatt, "and we'll gladly repair the damage; but you must know that this engine and his crew have prevented a serious accident. You and many others might have been badly hurt."

Sir Topham Hatt paused impressively. "It was a very close shave," he said.

"Oh!" said the barber. "Oh! Excuse me." He ran into his shop, fetched a basin of water, and washed Duck's face.

"I'm sorry, Duck," he said. "I didn't know you were being a brave engine."

"That's all right, Sir," said Duck. "I didn't know that either."

"You were very brave indeed," said Sir Topham Hatt kindly. "I'm proud of you. I shall tell 'City of Truro' about you the next time he comes."

"Oh, Sir!" Duck felt happier than he had been for weeks.

"And now," said Sir Topham Hatt, "when you are mended, you are coming home."

"Home, Sir? Do you mean the yard?"

"Of course."

"But, Sir, they don't like me. They like Diesel."

"Not now." Sir Topham Hatt smiled. "I never believed Diesel. After you went he told lies about Henry; so I sent him packing. The engines are sorry and want you back."

So, when a few days later he came home shining with new paint, there was a really rousing welcome for Duck the Great Western Engine.

Now flip the book over to start another Thomas & Friends adventure.